The Furry-Legged Teapot

retold by **Tim Myers**

illustrated by **Robert McGuire**

Marshall Cavendish Children

To Sister Mary Boniface, Sophie Bebb, Sam Gadd, Alex Blackburn, Tamiko Narita, and Nancy Roser—for
seeing the artist-tanuki in me, and not just the teapot
— T.M.

For Masami
—R.M.

Text copyright © 2007 by Tim Myers
Illustrations copyright © 2007 by Robert McGuire

Marshall Cavendish Corporation, 99 White Plains Road, Tarrytown, NY 10591
www.marshallcavendish.us

Library of Congress Cataloging-in-Publication Data
Myers, Tim (Tim Brian)
The furry-legged teapot : a unique retelling / by Tim Myers ; illustrated by Robert McGuire. — 1st ed.
p. cm.
Summary: In ancient Japan, a young tanuki, a raccoon-dog that can change shapes, becomes stuck in the form of a teapot. Includes notes on the
original Japanese folktale from which this story is derived.
ISBN-13: 978-0-7614-5295-9
[1. Magic—Fiction. 2. Foxes—Fiction. 3. Teapots—Fiction. 4. Japan—History—Fiction.] I. McGuire, Robert, 1978- ill. II. Title.
PZ7.M9919Fur 2007
[E]—dc22
2005016935

The text of this book is set in Meridien.
The illustrations are rendered in acrylic.
Book design by Vera Soki

Printed in Malaysia
First edition
1 3 5 6 4 2

Marshall Cavendish
Children

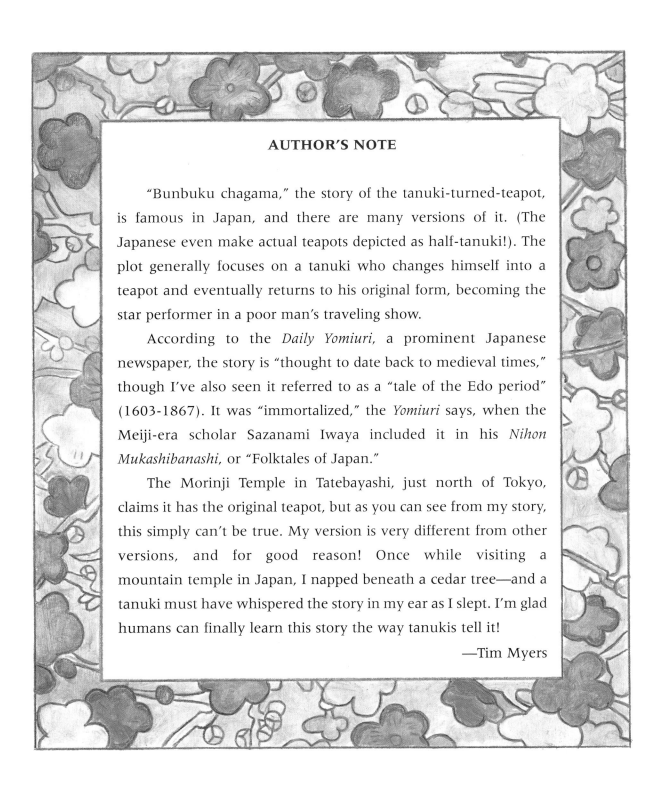

AUTHOR'S NOTE

"Bunbuku chagama," the story of the tanuki-turned-teapot, is famous in Japan, and there are many versions of it. (The Japanese even make actual teapots depicted as half-tanuki!). The plot generally focuses on a tanuki who changes himself into a teapot and eventually returns to his original form, becoming the star performer in a poor man's traveling show.

According to the *Daily Yomiuri*, a prominent Japanese newspaper, the story is "thought to date back to medieval times," though I've also seen it referred to as a "tale of the Edo period" (1603-1867). It was "immortalized," the *Yomiuri* says, when the Meiji-era scholar Sazanami Iwaya included it in his *Nihon Mukashibanashi*, or "Folktales of Japan."

The Morinji Temple in Tatebayashi, just north of Tokyo, claims it has the original teapot, but as you can see from my story, this simply can't be true. My version is very different from other versions, and for good reason! Once while visiting a mountain temple in Japan, I napped beneath a cedar tree—and a tanuki must have whispered the story in my ear as I slept. I'm glad humans can finally learn this story the way tanukis tell it!

—Tim Myers

A long time ago, a young tanuki named Yoshi lived with his family in the forests of the Joshin Mountains. Tanukis have powerful magic; they can even change themselves into objects or other beings. Yoshi couldn't wait to transform himself. But there was a lot to learn, and he often got impatient.

"Slowly, Yoshi-kun," his mother would say, and his father, and his grandparents, uncles, and aunts. "First work on concentration; changing comes later."

So Yoshi would try. But then he'd be distracted by a passing cloud or the smell of a fox, and nothing would happen. He knew his family offered advice because they loved him and wanted to help. But sometimes he felt like shouting, *Leave me alone! I can do it myself!*

Changing-power grows in tanukis as they get older. One day, as Yoshi watched a moon-white butterfly flitting past, he wished he could fly.

Suddenly—*puup!*—he was a butterfly! Wings trembling with excitement, he flew around a bit and came to rest on the mossy earth. *Puup!*—he was a tanuki again.

I can do it! he exulted.

Instantly he changed into a rock, then a blue snail, then a pine tree. *I've mastered it!* he told himself. So when he remembered the farm in the valley, he hurried off—for tanukis also love to play tricks on humans.

Peeking into the hut, he saw the farmer's wife at her chores. *I'll trick her!* he thought, and *puup!*—he was a teapot sitting beside the fire. But he hadn't thought of everything.

For just then the farmwife whisked up the teapot, filled it with water, and set it on the fire.

Yoshi began to feel heat running through him. *Oh no!* he thought, *I have to change back!* But the pain was so strong he couldn't concentrate. *Puup, puup, puup*—nothing happened! All he could do was pop out one leg.

When the farmwife saw a furry leg sticking out of her teapot, she screamed—*Aaaiiii!*

Grabbing the teapot, she rushed to the door and flung it as far as she could.

Yoshi was terrified, but managed to pop out two more legs. Wobbling off, he hid in the bushes. But he was too lonely and scared to really concentrate. Three legs was the best he could do—no head, tail, or body—and sometimes one of the legs would disappear and he'd topple over. And though he wouldn't admit it, what he wanted most was to be back with his family in his own burrow.

He knew he needed help, but he didn't dare return home. That would mean shame and dishonor. So at dawn he set off for the Morinji Temple. All the animals knew the monks, for those good men were followers of Buddha and kind to every living creature.

The monks were compassionate and generous—but they were only human. When they saw a furry-legged teapot galloping crookedly into their courtyard, they panicked. "A demon!" one cried. Another grabbed a broom and tried to swat Yoshi. Everyone was running and shouting. But Yoshi had nowhere else to go. So he dodged them as best he could, refusing to be driven away.

After a time the monks sat down panting. Yosin was exhausted, too, and lost *all* his concentration. Suddenly the teapot's legs disappeared, and it clanked onto the courtyard stones. The amazed monks carried the strange vessel to their abbot. He told them to lock it away.

When Yoshi woke hours later, he was nothing but a teapot in a dark room.

For many long months, this was his whole life. Again and again he tried to change back. But he missed his family terribly, and was too lonely and unsure of himself to focus his mind properly. Besides, he was constantly interrupted. The story of the furry-legged teapot had spread through the land, and many came to see this marvel. He never knew when the door might suddenly open and visitors would come crowding in. Then he'd rush around trying to yell, *Help me! I can't change back!* But the people would only stare at the amazing teapot with legs.

And although Yoshi yearned for a smiling face or a loving touch, the monks weren't kind to him. Why should they be? To them he was only a teapot, and perhaps a demon-teapot at that! This made him even lonelier, which made concentrating even harder.

I'll never be a tanuki again, he moaned to himself.

One spring day, when Yoshi could smell the rain-wet fields beyond the monastery, he heard the monks calling to one another. The Emperor himself was coming to see the teapot, all the way from Kyoto! Yoshi felt honored and excited. Surely the Son of the Gods would help him.

The monks took him to the courtyard, where the Emperor could examine him in sunlight. First a great crowd of lords, ladies, servants, and samurai streamed through the gates. Then bearers in purple and gold carried in the Emperor's palanquin. When the Emperor finally stepped forth in a cloud of iridescent silk, Yoshi's heart beat fast. The Emperor spoke with the abbot and looked the teapot over. On that day it was just a little furry. Then he turned to go, having seen all he wanted.

Even he *can't do anything!* Yoshi thought bitterly.

But as the Emperor bent to enter his palanquin, a small voice called out, "Grandfather—may I see the teapot too?"

The Emperor stood straight again and smiled. "Of course, Grandson!" he exclaimed, as a little boy came bounding out of a smaller palanquin behind his. "I'd forgotten! Come, child, come and look."

The boy knelt on the paving stones. All was quiet as he looked Yoshi over. Then the boy said, "Grandfather, this isn't a teapot."

Everyone gasped. Was the Emperor's grandson weak in the mind? Anyone could see it was a teapot!

"But, Grandson, look again," said the Emperor patiently. "See the spout and the handle, the flat bottom and the opening for water? This is a teapot."

"Oji-san," the boy said politely, "people told me this was a teapot with tanuki legs. But I think it's a tanuki turning into a teapot."

Again everyone gasped. Could the child be right?

The boy picked the teapot up and began stroking it as if it were a puppy. "Do you like being scratched, Tanuki-kun?" he whispered. "Does that feel nice? Oh, you must miss your family. . . ."

I do! Yoshi thought. For the first time since he became a teapot, someone was being kind to him. He glowed with happiness. Even through his teapot body he could feel the boy's warm fingers. *Ooooooooohhh*, he purred, as his mind grew very calm and focused.

But then—something felt different.

Could it be . . . ?!

The people cried out in astonishment. Before their very eyes, the teapot had become a young tanuki! It was lying asleep in the Emperor's grandson's arms. At the noise of the crowd, it jumped to the pavement and looked around wildly.

"Capture it!" someone shouted, but the Emperor cried, "No!" Everyone froze.

"Grandson," the Emperor said softly, "what should be done with this teapot-tanuki?"

"Let it go!" the little boy pleaded.

The Emperor turned to his guards. "Form a passageway," he ordered. Yoshi watched, unbelieving, as the samurai stepped aside. Beyond the last soldier he could glimpse fields and trees, and his heart almost burst with joy.

Looking up at the Emperor and his grandson, Yoshi quickly bowed. Then he ran off between the samurai as fast as he could scamper. He didn't breathe again till he felt warm earth and pine needles beneath his feet.

When he came at last to his family's burrow, they all looked up—and their eyes grew huge.

"Yoshi!" they shouted. "You've come home!"

And now he understood. *I have to learn things for myself*, he thought. *But without love and kindness, I can't concentrate and do my best. I need my family around me.*

Father and mother, brothers and sisters, grandparents, uncles, aunts, and cousins all came tumbling over him, laughing and calling his name.

And he knew he'd never have to be a teapot again.